# THE
# GHOST'S DINNER

By Jacques Duquennoy

AN ARTISTS & WRITERS GUILD BOOK
Golden Books
Western Publishing Company, Inc.

Henry has invited his friends to a dinner party.

When Henry's guests arrive,
he is still cooking in the kitchen.

"Would you like some juice before dinner?"
he asks his friends.
"Yes!" they all answer at the same time.

"Uh-oh," says Henry, "the tray is stuck.

There. That's the way to do it."

"These juices are so colorful," Jack says. "Yes," says Henry. "I have passion fruit, sour cherry, very berry, lemonade, and spinach juice."

"Here. Try the spinach juice."

"It's not bad!    In fact, it's delicious."

"Look at us.

We're so colorful!"

"Now I can serve dinner," Henry tells his guests.

"First we'll have pumpkin soup. But be careful," Henry warns. "The soup is very hot."

Henry's guests love the soup.

Some have seconds.

Then they eat salmon

and salad

and cheese.

"I have a very special dessert,"
Henry tells his friends. "I'll bring it in."

"Here it is. I hope you like it."

"Mmmm. This looks good.
But what is it?" asks Jack.

"It's my secret ghost dessert recipe," says Henry.

"It's magic."

"Amazing! I can't see you anymore."

"Where did everybody go?"

"I'm clearing the table."

"Okay. Let's take the dirty dishes into the kitchen."
"Be careful," says Henry. "Don't trip."

"Now let's wash the dishes

and dry them."

"I think it's time for hot chocolate," says Henry.

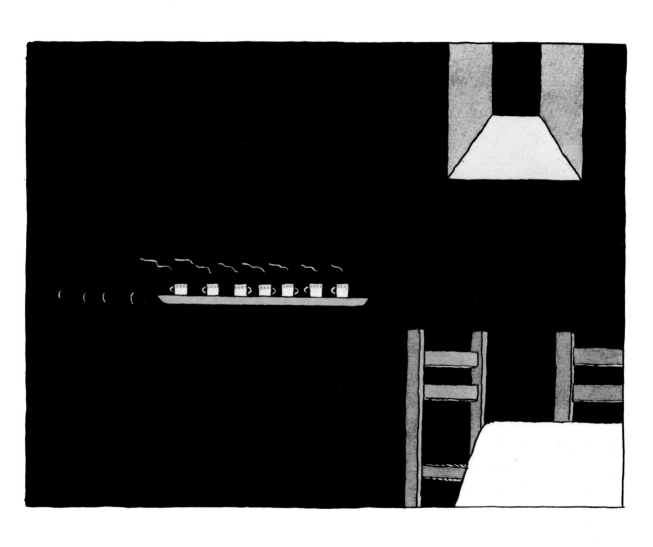

"This is delicious.

But now look at us. What shall we do?"

"I know," says Henry. "Let's drink some milk."

And they do.

"But where's Henry?"

"Maybe he's still in the kitchen," says Arthur. "Henry? Are you in there?"

"BOO!"

The perfect end to the ghost's dinner.

Library of Congress Cataloging-in-Publication Data
Duquennoy, Jacques.
The ghost's dinner / by Jacques Duquennoy.
p.     cm.
"First published in 1994 by Albin Michel Jeunesse, France"—
T.p. verso.
Summary: Henry the Ghost hosts a dinner party
at which the ghost guests turn the colors of the
foods they eat.
ISBN 0-307-17510-3 (hardcover): $9.95
[1. Ghosts—Fiction. 2. Color—Fiction.
I. Title.
PZ7.D92845Gh  1994[E]—dc20  93-32767  CIP  AC